Words to Know Before You Read

Let's Learn The **Zz** Sound

Zac

zebra

zero

zigzag

zip line

Zoe

zombies

zoo

zookeeper

www.rourkeeducationalmedia.com

Edited by Precious McKenzie
Illustrated by Louise Anglicas
Art Direction and Page Layout by Tara Raymo
Cover Design by Renee Brady

Library of Congress PCN Data

Zoom to the Zoo / Luana Mitten
ISBN 978-1-62169-245-4 (hard cover) (alk. paper)
ISBN 978-1-62169-203-4 (soft cover)
Library of Congress Control Number: 2012952741

Rourke Educational Media
Printed in the United States of America,
North Mankato, Minnesota

rourkeeducationalmedia.com
customerservice@rourkeeducationalmedia.com • PO Box 643328 Vero Beach, Florida 32964

ZOOM to the ZOO

Counselor Nixi

Viv

Ollie

Counselor Quinn

Zoe

Rodney

Jack

Written By Luana K. Mitten

Illustrated By Louise Anglicas

"Let's zoom to the zoo," calls Counselor Quinn.

CAMP ADVENTURE

"Hold on tight," cautions Counselor Nixi.

The bus zigs and it zags as it zooms to the zoo.

"We're here!" says Counselor Quinn.

"What a wild ride," says Counselor Nixi.

"I can't wait to see the zebras!" calls Ollie.

"Do you think there are babies?" asks Zoe.

"We will soon see," says Counselor Nixi.

Rodney says, "Wow! The zoo has a zip line. Let's zip down the line on our way to the zebras."

So one-by-one they zigzag as they zip down the line.

"This zoo is fun!" says Jack as he lands.

"But where are the zebras?" Ollie demands.

"Look at the map," says Counselor Quinn.

ZOO MAP

EXIT

15

If we zigzag right and then zigzag left, we'll be at the zebras.

So we zig and we zag and we zigzag again.

"Oh no!" cries Ollie. "There are zero zebras!"

Viv says, "Maybe they were zapped by zombies!"

"Oh, it's nothing like that," laughs Zookeeper Zac.

We all follow Zookeeper Zac through the door and guess what we see fast asleep on the floor?

After Reading Word Study
Picture Glossary

Directions: Look at each picture and read the definition. Then write a list of all of the words you know that start with the same sound as zebra. Remember to look in the book for more words.

zebra (ZEE-bruh): A zebra is an animal like a horse. It has black and white stripes.

zero (ZEER-oh): Zero is a numeral that is written like this 0. Zero means nothing or none.

zigzag (zig-ZAG): When you zigzag, you move making short, sharp turns.

zip line (ZIP LINE): A zip line is a line with a pulley. You hold onto the pulley to slide down the line.

zombies (ZOM-beez): Zombies are imaginary, scary looking people. They are not real.

zoo (ZOO): A zoo is a garden or park where wild animals live. People visit zoos to learn about the animals.

zookeeper (ZOO-kee-pur): A zookeeper takes care of the animals living in a zoo.

About the Author

Luana Mitten lives in Tampa with her family. They all like zipping over to Busch Gardens where there are zillions of zebras and rides that zigzag, zip, and zoom!

Ask The Author!
www.rem4students.com

About the Illustrator

Louise Anglicas is a Manchester born illustrator now living in the Staffordshire Potteries with her partner and two young daughters. Her first job was as a ceramic designer which involved reading Harry Potter books, and then designing mugs and children's breakfast sets based on them! Louise loves to travel with her family. Her favorite thing to do on holiday is go to waterparks with very big slides!

24